WITHDRAWN

Baldwinsville
33 East Genesee St.
Baldwinsville, NY 13027-2575

MAY 14 2008

WITHDRAWN

The BLOCK MESS MONSTER

Baldwinsville Public Library
33 East Genesee Street
Baldwinsville, NY 13027-2575
WITHDRAWN

Betsy Howie

Illustrated by C. B. Decker

HENRY HOLT AND COMPANY · NEW YORK

Henry Holt and Company, LLC
Publishers since 1866
175 Fifth Avenue
New York, New York 10010
www.HenryHoltKids.com

Henry Holt® is a registered trademark of Henry Holt and Company, LLC.
Text copyright © 2008 by Betsy Howie
Illustrations copyright © 2008 by C. B. Decker
All rights reserved.
Distributed in Canada by H. B. Fenn and Company Ltd.

AUG 1 4 2008

Library of Congress Cataloging-in-Publication Data
Howie, Betsy.
The Block Mess Monster / Betsy Howie ; illustrated by C. B. Decker.—1st ed.
p.   cm.
Summary: Calpurnia has tried to explain that the huge and scary monster that lives in her
room does not want the room cleaned but her mother, who cannot see the monster, has a
few ideas about how to make it go away.
ISBN-13: 978-0-8050-7940-1 / ISBN-10: 0-8050-7940-8
[1. Monsters—Fiction. 2. Orderliness—Fiction. 3. Mothers and daughters—Fiction.]
I. Decker, Cynthia B., ill. II. Title.
PZ7.H8398Blo 2008   [E]—dc22   2007007229

First Edition—2008 / Designed by Amelia May Anderson
Printed in China on acid-free paper. ∞
10 9 8 7 6 5 4 3 2 1

For CAC
—B. H.

For Ada, Ruth, and Elianna—
monsters of a different sort
—C. B. D.

I am Calpurnia.

The lady over there, folding the laundry,
that is my mom.

That really big, really scary thing in my room
right there, that is the Block Mess Monster.

"Clean up your room, Calpurnia!"
(That's what my mom keeps saying.)

"But there's a monster!"
(That's what I keep saying.)

The Block Mess Monster does not want me
to put him away.

My mom does.
This is a problem.

Mom does not see the Block Mess Monster.

But the Block Mess Monster sees her.

That is another problem.

"Just say POOF!"
(Mom says that all the time.)

She thinks POOF! makes
monsters go away.

It does not. I will show you.

"POOF!"

I say.

"Is it gone?" she says.

"NO!" I say.

"It did not work."

"Then do a double

POOF!" she says.

"Mommy!"

"Goodness gracious,
Calpurnia!"
(Mom always says that.)
"There is *no* monster. . . .

"See?" Mom says.

"No monster."

"NO!"

I scream.

He does not like it when she picks up my room.

I've had to save her many times.

Sometimes I think she does not appreciate what I have done for her.

"Where are you going?" I ask her.

"I have to do the vacuuming," she says.

"But the monster!" I say.

"Calpurnia!" she says.
"I'm losing my patience."

Oh, great. Now there are two monsters.

"Okay," Mom says.
"I have an idea."

"What?" I ask.

"Maybe we could get the monster to help clean up your room," Mom says.

"Where is his head?"
Mom asks.

"At the end of his neck," I say.
(Sometimes I wonder if Mom
needs glasses.)

"Hello, Monster," Mom says.
"Would you like to climb up onto
the shelf?"

And do you know what? Mom took the monster's hand, and it hopped on the shelf and disappeared!

Sometimes it's hard for Mom to pay attention. But when she finally does, she comes up with the best ideas.